Rachel Armitage is originally from Wolverhampton and is a former magazine and newspaper journalist. She lives in rural Lincolnshire with her husband and two children. This is her debut children's book.

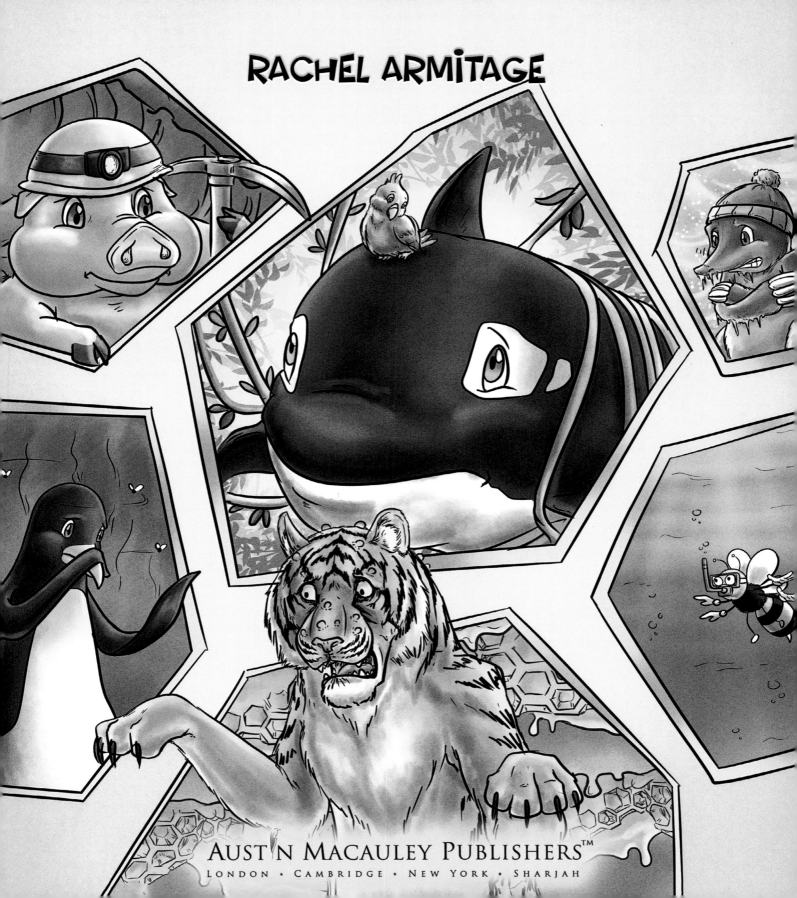

We Don't Live There!

RACHEL ARMITAGE

AUSTIN MACAULEY PUBLISHERS™
LONDON · CAMBRIDGE · NEW YORK · SHARJAH

A CIP catalogue record for this title is available from the British Library.

ISBN 9781528980319 (Paperback)
ISBN 9781398421585 (ePub e-book)

www.austinmacauley.com

First Published 2021
Austin Macauley Publishers Ltd®
1 Canada Square
Canary Wharf
London
E14 5AA

This book would never have happened without Kev, and my dear old dad, the most bostin' blokes of all. Ta muchly.

Thank you to the Hubberts for their advice, feedback and endless gin.
Chin chin!

To the amazing girls in the village who always listened, never judged and were always there. You rock!

And most importantly, to my babies, Isla Bear and Rory Spud. This is for you.

Down under the sea where it's deep, blue and clear,
The bee swims along in a swarm far and near.
He's going chasing after fish to have a quick bite,
But, hang on, a bee underwater doesn't look right...

"Help!" cries the bee, with a yell and a shout,
"I don't live here, it's too wet, get me out!"

And who's that down in Antarctica? Why, it's Mr Mole!
Catching fish with his mouth and swallowing them whole,
He plods the ice with his friends and family,
But without warm feathers, he's finding it rather chilly.

"Help!" cries the mole, with a yell and a shout,
"I don't live here, it's too cold, get me out!"

Who's that stripy creature mooching around in the hive?
Why it's a bold, fierce tiger – snakes alive!
He's collecting pollen to make yummy honey,
But a tiger squashed into that hive just isn't funny.

"Help!" cries the tiger, with a yell and a shout,
"I don't live here, it's too small, get me out!"

Now what about the penguin sat in the sty?
He loves munching fruit under the deep blue sky.
You'll often see him rolling around the stinky mud bath,
Wait – penguins don't live on farms, don't be daft!

"Help!" cries the penguin, with a yell and a shout,
"I don't live here, it's too muddy, get me out!"

This fine fellow is the pig in his underground house,
Sniffing out wriggly worms to share with the mouse.
He pushes up molehills and the gardeners are in a rage,
But a pig underground is a little bit strange.

"Help!" cries the pig, with a yell and a shout,
"I don't live here, it's too dark, get me out!"

Then there's the whale hanging out in the jungle,
Prowling through the undergrowth with never a grumble.
He's roaring and running after his tasty prey,
But how can a whale run without any legs, I hear you say.

"Help!" cries the whale, with a yell and a shout,
"I don't live here, it's too dry, get me out!"

Well this isn't right, we've got it all wrong!
Bees can't swim and moles in the sea don't belong!
Poor penguin is in the wrong habitat,
And a whale on land – we can't have that.

Just look at those grumpy and confused faces,
Let's put these animals back in their proper places.
Who belongs in the hive and who should be in the sty?
You tell me who lives where, and why.

And down in Antarctica is where the penguin should be,
Not the sty where it's terribly muddy and smelly.
Penguins love to dive in the sea for a swim,
But being stuck in the mud? Well, life would be grim.

And it's the whale who belongs in the sea,
Diving through the waves is the place to be.
Whales need water or life wouldn't be fun,
And off he goes, there's hunting to be done.

So who lives in the sty? It's the pig obviously,

He couldn't fit in the mole's hole, don't be silly.

With his large backside he'd get stuck and wouldn't budge,

He's much happier in the mud, muck and sludge.

Back into the hive is where the bee should go,

Of course a bee can't swim, oh no no no!

His job is to fly and collect pollen from flowers,

For a bee to swim, he'd need magical powers!

It's far too cold on the ice for a tiny wee mole,
They belong underground in a deep, dark hole.
Moley can't see very well, he likes it where it's cosy,
And instead of fish, a nice juicy worm for his tea.

And in the jungle, last but not least,
Lives the tiger, the most magnificent of beasts.
Never mind being squashed into that tiny beehive,
A big cat out hunting has never felt more alive.

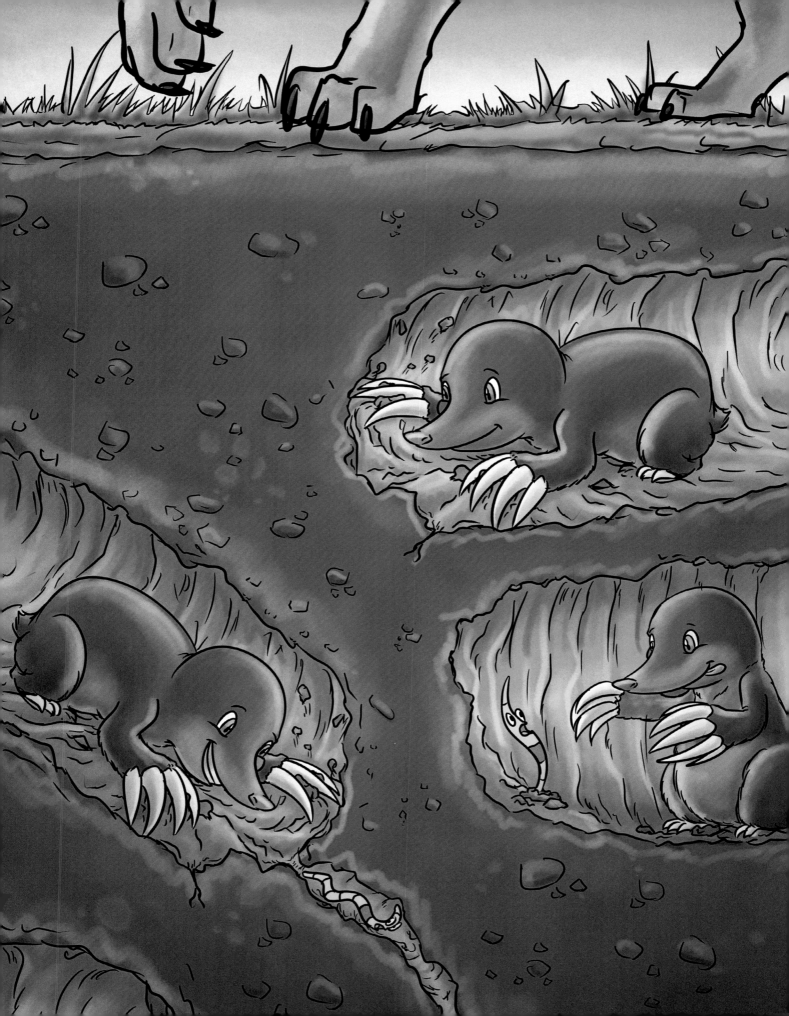

Now everyone is back safely where they should be,
The animals are in their proper homes and are
finally happy.
So if you ever see a mole in the sea or a pig in a tree,
Better get help and take them home – hurry, hurry!